JUST ME
AND MY PUPPY

BY
MERCER MAYER

*For Roger Buoy,
who's always wanted
a puppy of his very own.*

A Random House PICTUREBACK® Book

Random House 🏠 **New York**

Just Me and My Puppy book, characters, text, and images © 1985 Mercer Mayer. LITTLE CRITTER, MERCER MAYER'S LITTLE CRITTER, and MERCER MAYER'S LITTLE CRITTER and Logo are registered trademarks of Orchard House Licensing Company. All rights reserved. Published in the United States by Random House Children's Books, a division of Random House, Inc., New York. Originally published in 1985 by Golden Books Publishing Company, Inc. PICTUREBACK, RANDOM HOUSE, and the Random House colophon are registered trademarks of Random House, Inc.
www.randomhouse.com/kids
Educators and librarians, for a variety of teaching tools, visit us at
www.randomhouse.com/teachers
Library of Congress Control Number: 84-82601
ISBN-13: 978-0-307-11937-7   ISBN-10: 0-307-11937-8
Printed in the United States of America
25 24
First Random House Edition 2006

I wanted a puppy, just for me.
So I traded my baseball mitt for one.

My baby sister liked him
right away.

And, boy, were Mom and Dad surprised!
They said I could keep him if I took
care of him myself.

So I am taking very good care
of my puppy.
I feed him in the morning.

He eats every bite.

Then I put on his leash and
we go for a walk.

I am teaching my puppy
how to heel.

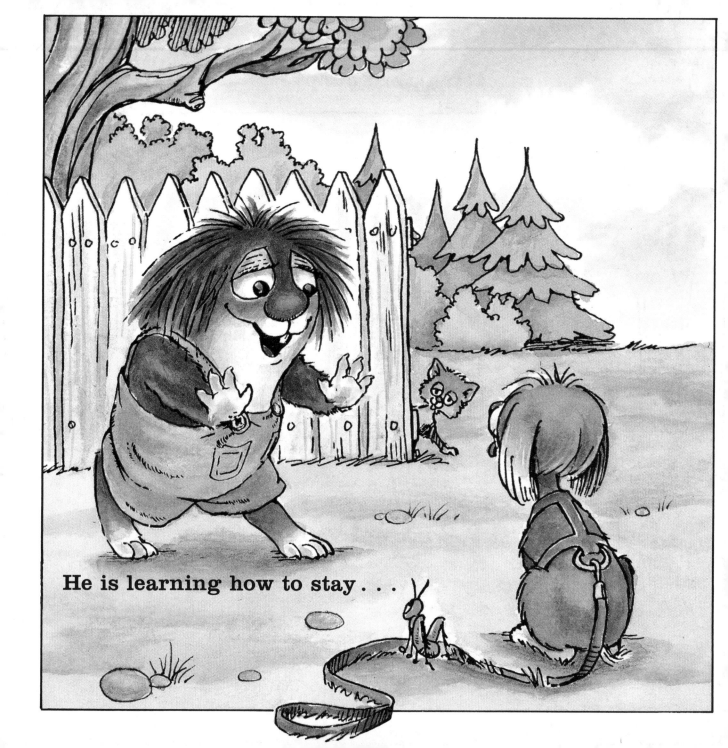

He is learning how to stay. . . .

. . . except when he sees a cat.

. . . and how to roll over.

He still needs some practice.

But he already knows how to fetch.

My puppy is a big help around the house.

He's a good guard dog.

He brings in
the paper
for my dad.

And he keeps me company
while I do my homework.

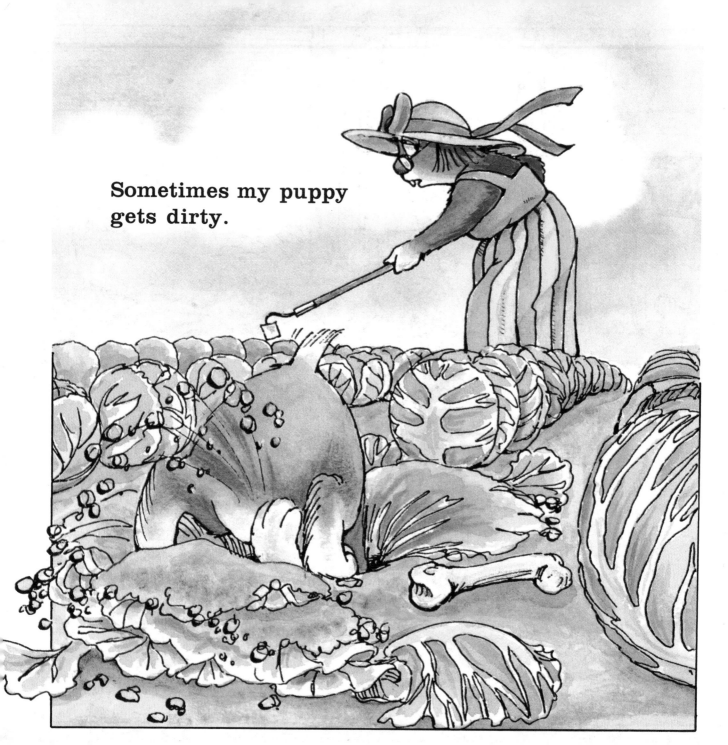

Sometimes my puppy
gets dirty.

Then I give him a bath.

I get him nice and dry
so he won't catch a cold.

Then we get ready for bed . . .

. . . just me and my puppy.